AUBERRY

WITHDRAWN
WORN, SOILED, OBSOLETE

Auberry
SEP 11 1986

X
398.2
G131th

Galdone, Paul.
The three sillies / by Joseph Jacobs ; retold and illustrated by Paul Galdone. -- New York : Clarion Books/Ticknor & Fields, c1981.
1 v. (unpaged) : ill. ; 27 cm.

Summary: A young man believes his sweetheart and her family are the three silliest people in the world until he meets three others who are even sillier.
ISBN 0-395-30172-6 : $9.95

1. Folklore--England. I. Jacobs, Joseph, 1854-1916./Three sillies. II. Title.

9

1010908620

831003
EO /EF

831003 CF
83-B6251
80-22197/AC

THE Three Sillies

BY JOSEPH JACOBS

Retold and Illustrated by

PAUL GALDONE

CLARION BOOKS
TICKNOR & FIELDS : A HOUGHTON MIFFLIN COMPANY
NEW YORK

To B. B. at F. M. L.

Clarion Books, 52 Vanderbilt Avenue, New York, N. Y. 10017
Copyright © 1981 by Paul Galdone. All rights reserved.
Printed in the U. S. A.

Library of Congress Cataloging in Publication Data
Galdone, Paul. The three sillies.
Summary: A young man believes his sweetheart and her family are the three silliest people in the world until he meets three others who are even sillier.
[1. Folklore—England] I. Jacobs, Joseph, 1854-1916.
Three sillies. II. Title. PZ8.1.G15Th 398.2'0941
[E] 80-22197 ISBN 0-395-30172-6

ONCE upon a time there was a farmer and his wife who had one daughter, and this daughter was soon to be married to a young gentleman.

Often the young man came to supper at the farmhouse and the daughter would be sent down into the cellar to get a pitcher of cider.

One evening, as she was waiting for the pitcher to fill, she happened to glance up at the ceiling and saw an axe stuck into one of the beams above her head. Though it must have been there a long time, somehow she had never noticed it before and she began thinking.

"Suppose my young man and I were to be married," she thought, "and we were to have a son, and he was to grow up and be sent down here to get cider as I am doing now, and suppose that axe was to fall on his head—"

"What a dreadful thing that would be!"

And she sat down on a bench and began to sob.

Upstairs they began to wonder why it was taking her so long to get the cider, so her mother went down to look. There she found the daughter crying and the cider running all over the floor.

"Whatever is the matter?" said the mother.

"Oh, Mother!" said the daughter, "Look at that horrid axe!"

"What of it?" said her mother.

"Well, suppose my young man and I were to be married, and suppose we had a son. And suppose he was to grow up and be sent down here to get cider. And suppose that axe was to fall on his head—"

"What a dreadful thing that would be!"

"Oh, dreadful, dreadful!" said the mother, and she sat down beside her daughter and started crying, too.

After a bit the father began to wonder why his wife and daughter hadn't come back.

He went down into the cellar to look and there the two sat crying, with the cider running all over the floor.

"Whatever is the matter?" said the father.

"Look at that horrid axe!" said the mother.

"What of it?" said the father.

"Just suppose if our daughter and her sweetheart were to be married, and suppose they had a son. And suppose he was to grow up, and suppose he was to come down into the cellar to get cider. And suppose that axe was to fall on his head—"

"What a dreadful thing that would be!"

"Oh, dreadful, dreadful!" said the father, and he sat down beside his wife and daughter, and started crying, too.

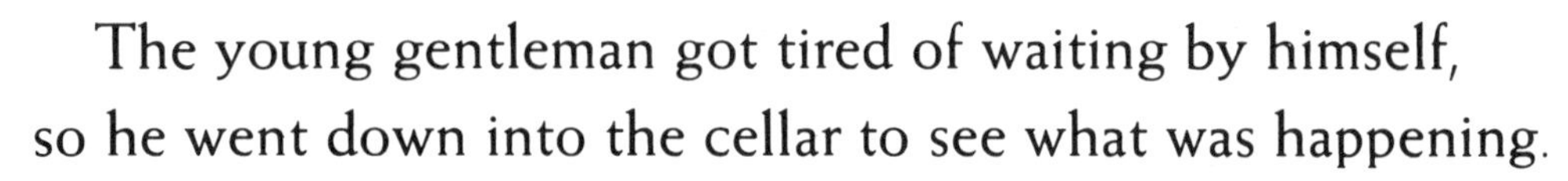

The young gentleman got tired of waiting by himself, so he went down into the cellar to see what was happening.

There the three sat crying side by side, with the cider running all over the floor.

The young man went straight over and turned off the tap. Then he said,

"Whatever are you three doing, sitting there crying, and letting the cider run all over the floor?"

"Oh," said the father, "look at that horrid axe!"

"What of it?" said the young man.

"Well, suppose you and our daughter were to be married, and suppose you were to have a son."

"And suppose he was to grow up and was to come down into the cellar to get cider and suppose that axe was to fall on his head— What a dreadful thing that would be!"

The young gentleman burst out laughing.

Then he pulled the axe from the beam and said,

"I've traveled many miles, but I've never met three such big sillies as you before. Now I shall start out on my travels again. When I can find three bigger sillies than you three, then I'll come back and we will have a wedding."

So, still laughing, the young gentleman set out on his journey.

And the three sillies cried harder than ever because he had left them.

The young man traveled a long way into the country. At last he came to a cottage that had grass growing on the roof. The old woman who lived there was trying to get her cow to climb up a ladder to the roof, but the poor thing would not go.

"What are you trying to do?" asked the young man.

"See that beautiful grass?" said the old woman. "I'm going to get the cow up on the roof so she can eat it."

"Oh, you poor silly!" said the young gentleman. "You should cut the grass and throw it down to the cow!"

But the old woman insisted it would be easier to get the cow up the ladder than to get the grass down. So the young man helped her push and coax the cow up onto the roof.

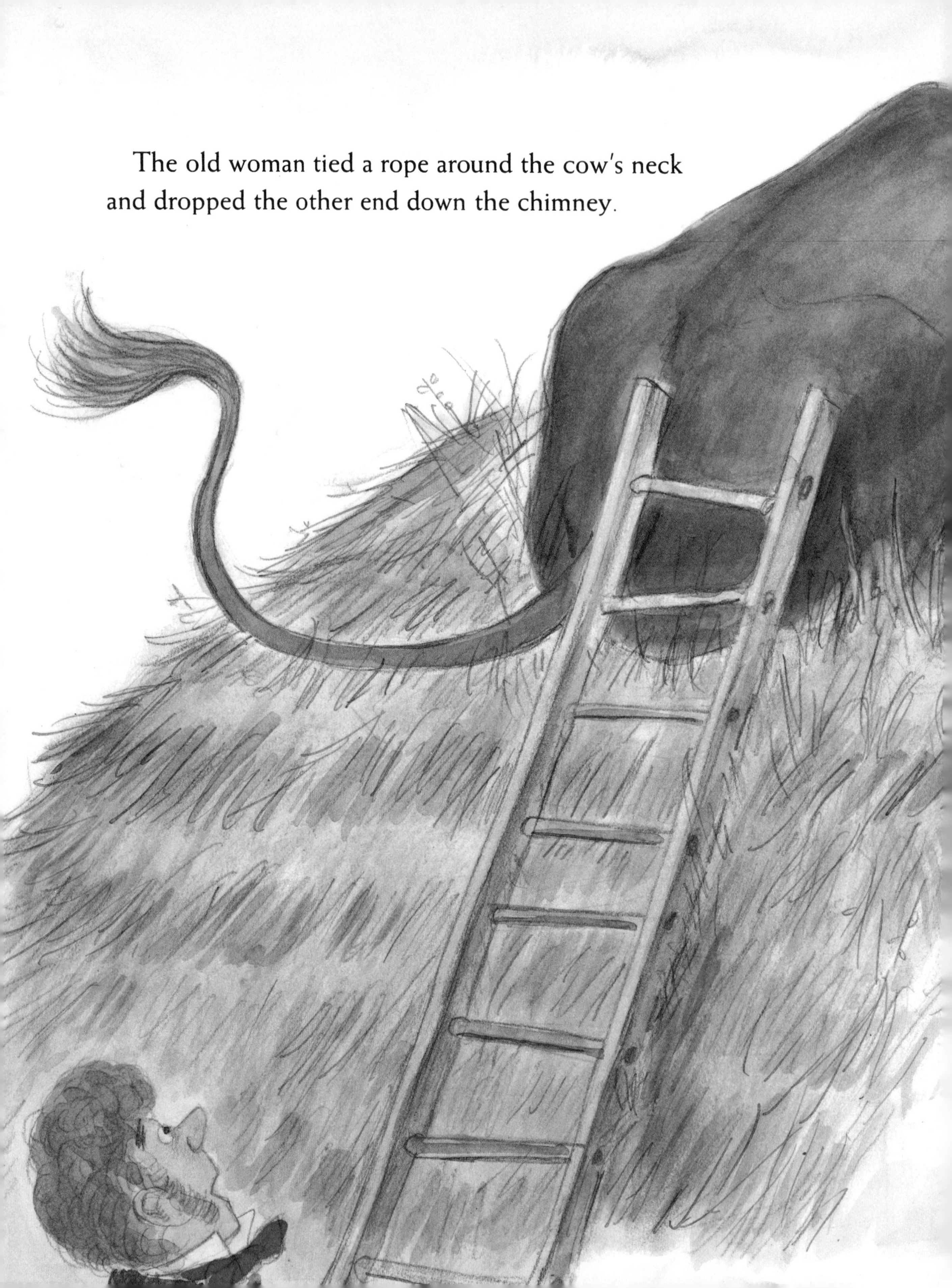

The old woman tied a rope around the cow's neck and dropped the other end down the chimney.

Then she climbed quickly down the ladder.

"What are you going to do now?" asked the young man.

"Why, I shall tie the other end of the rope around my waist, so the cow can't fall off the roof without my knowing it!" said the old woman. And she ran into her cottage.

Scarcely had the old woman tied the rope around her waist when—whoosh—the cow slid off the roof. DOWN went the cow. . .

. . . and UP went the old woman!
She shot up the chimney
among clouds
of black soot.

If the young gentleman hadn't cut the rope
and lowered her down, she would be there yet.

"Well, that's one big silly," the young man said to himself as he went on his way.

He traveled on and on until he finally stopped at an inn for the night. They were so full at the inn that he had to share a room with another traveler.

The other man was a very pleasant fellow and the two of them passed the night comfortably.

But in the morning, when they were both getting dressed, the young gentleman was surprised to see the other man hang his trousers on the knobs of the chest of drawers.

Then the man ran across the room
and tried to jump into them.

He tried it over and over again while the young man watched in amazement. At last he stopped.

"Oh, dear," the man said, gasping for breath. "I do think trousers are the most awkward kind of clothes that ever were. It takes me the best part of an hour to get into mine every morning, and I get so hot! How do you manage yours?"

The young gentleman couldn't help laughing. Then he showed the man how to put on his trousers in the usual way.

"Well, that's a second big silly," the young man said to himself as he went on his way.

That evening he came to a village, and outside the village there was a big pond.

A crowd of people was reaching into the pond with rakes, and brooms, and pitchforks.

"What is the matter?" asked the young gentleman.

"The moon has fallen into the pond," the people said. "And we can't get it out."

The young gentleman laughed.
"Look up into the sky," he said.

"There's the moon. It's only her reflection in the water."

But the people wouldn't listen to him. They screamed at him, and shook their fists, and waved their pitchforks.

The young man ran away from them as fast as he could. "Those people are certainly the silliest sillies in all the world!" he said to himself as he ran.

Then he smiled. "I guess my own three sillies back home are not so silly after all."

So the young man went home and married his own dear silly, and if they didn't live happily ever after, that's nothing to do with you or me.

FRESNO COUNTY FREE LIBRARY COPY 9